ECOSYSTEMS

Written by Claire Daniel

STECK-VAUGHN
A Harcourt Company

www.steck-vaughn.com

CONTENTS

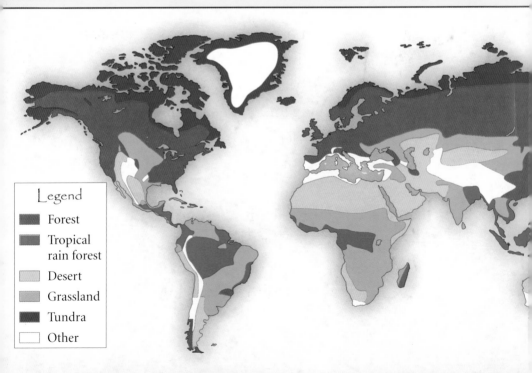

Legend
- Forest
- Tropical rain forest
- Desert
- Grassland
- Tundra
- Other

CHAPTER 1
WHAT IS AN ECOSYSTEM?

In cold weather people use heating systems to warm homes and offices. Cars stop because they have brake systems. Bus systems take people to all parts of a city. A system is a group of parts that work together. Some systems include only nonliving parts. For example, a home computer system might have a hard drive, a video monitor, and a printer. None of these parts is alive.

Nature has systems, too. An **ecosystem** is a group of living and nonliving things that are found together in nature. A desert is one kind of ecosystem. A grassland is another. The nonliving things in ecosystems include soil, water, light, air, and minerals, such as iron. The living things in ecosystems include animals and plants. Each part of an ecosystem is needed in order for the system to stay the same.

PHOTOSYNTHESIS

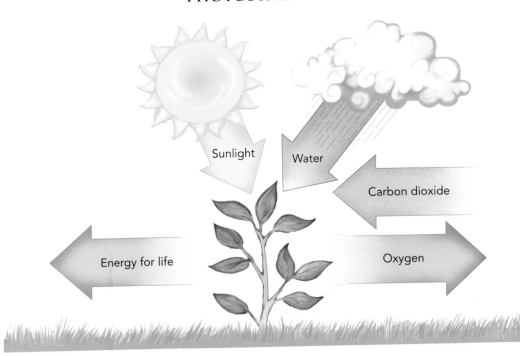

Sunlight

Water

Carbon dioxide

Energy for life

Oxygen

Green plants use sunlight, water, and carbon dioxide from the air to make their own food. The making of food is called **photosynthesis**.

When scientists talk about ecosystems, they say that energy flows through them. The flow of energy connects the living and nonliving parts. The energy in almost all ecosystems starts with light energy from the sun. Plants use the sun's light energy to make a kind of sugar. They use the sugar as their food.

Scientists call plants **producers** because they can produce, or make, their own food. When an animal eats a plant, it takes in the plant's energy. Animals that eat plants are called **consumers**. Animals that eat other animals are consumers, too. Other living things called **decomposers** break down dead consumers and wastes.

Scientists keep track of the energy in an ecosystem by studying its food chains. A food chain shows who eats whom. Imagine the sun and a plant with seeds on it. A mouse eats the seeds. The next day, a weasel eats the mouse. That night, an owl swoops down and eats the weasel. When the owl dies, its body returns to the earth.

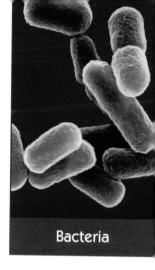

Bacteria

Fungi

Bacteria, fungi, and animals such as the dung beetle are all decomposers.

Dung beetles

A FOREST FOOD CHAIN

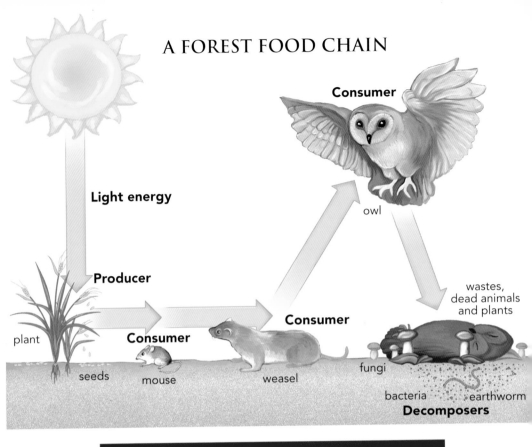

Light energy

Producer

Consumer

Consumer

Consumer

plant

seeds

mouse

weasel

owl

fungi

bacteria   earthworm

Decomposers

wastes,
dead animals
and plants

In a food chain, energy flows from the sun
and through the producers, consumers, and
decomposers.

Bacteria and other decomposers break down the body
into **nutrients** that other living things need.

As energy moves through an ecosystem, much of it is
lost. For example, a mouse keeps only about one tenth
of the energy stored in plant seeds. What happens to
the other nine tenths? The mouse can't break down

some of the energy in the seeds. The mouse uses some of the energy to live, and it loses some as heat that comes off its body. The same thing happens with every consumer in a food chain.

Unlike energy, nutrients flow through an ecosystem again and again. This circular movement is called a cycle. Rain washes away some of the nutrients into streams. Some of the nutrients stay in the soil and make it richer. Then plants can use the nutrients to grow. Decomposers are an important part of many nutrient cycles. They break down dead things and waste so that the nutrients in them can return to the soil, water, or air.

CHAPTER 2
THE FOREST ECOSYSTEM

Deep in western Europe, the last drops of an early morning rain drip slowly off the broad leaf of an oak tree. In a little clearing, a fox watches a rabbit closely, looking for its next meal.

The odors of rotting wood and damp soil rise from the dark brown earth. A great spotted woodpecker doesn't notice. Looking for insects, it busily pecks a hollow in the oak, then flies away.

No one can see the oak's roots stretching deep inside the earth. No one can hear the earthworm burrowing into the rich, damp soil. No one knows that the young of the woodpecker sleep in their nest inside the tree. For now, the forest is quiet, ready for the day to come.

Tons of leaves fall to the floor of a deciduous forest.

Trees are the main living things in a forest. Trees in some forests lose their leaves in the fall. Such trees are called **deciduous** trees. They are also called hardwoods because their wood is strong and hard. A deciduous forest contains deciduous trees such as oak, hickory, beech, birch, maple, and elm.

The leaves of deciduous trees are wide and flat so that they can better catch the sunlight. The leaves of some of these trees turn bright colors before they fall. In spring, buds form on the branches and grow into the leaves of summer. Deciduous trees do most of their growing in the spring. Even though a young deciduous tree has wide, flat leaves, it cannot grow in the shade of its parent. Young trees that grow into adults need places with lots of sunlight.

The leaves of deciduous trees form a cover, or canopy, at the top of the forest. Shrubs, bushes, and other kinds of small trees grow below the canopy. On the forest floor lie dead leaves, twigs, and branches that have fallen off the trees. Mosses grow on and around the rotting twigs and branches. Worms eat the fallen leaves on the forest floor and leave behind waste. Then fungi and bacteria eat the worm's waste. The wastes from the fungi and bacteria then enter the soil, making it rich.

Why Do Leaves Turn Colors?

The leaves of trees use **chlorophyll** to capture the sunlight they need to make their own food. Chlorophyll reflects green light, so tree leaves look green to us in summer. The temperature drop that comes in autumn causes the chlorophyll to break down. When the chlorophyll disappears, the red, brown, and yellow colors of the leaves appear.

Ponds are an important part of the forest ecosystem.

A deciduous forest has many different food chains. For example, grasshoppers eat plants, and bluebirds eat the grasshoppers. In a forest where oak trees **thrive,** squirrels eat the acorns. Foxes, hawks, and owls depend on squirrels for food. What about the worms that eat the rotting leaves? Moles eat the worms. Snakes eat the moles, and hawks eat the snakes.

A deciduous forest needs at least 16 inches (40 centimeters) of rain per year in order for the trees to survive. Some of this rain is used by the trees. Some of it falls into ponds and lakes, where it is drunk by animals.

The Water Cycle

Water is a nonliving part of an ecosystem. A deciduous forest gets a lot of water. That is one reason why it has so much plant life. Where does this water come from? Where does this water go?

The sun starts the water cycle. The sun heats up the water in ponds, lakes, rivers, and oceans. The sun also heats up the water in plants, soil, and living things. This water **evaporates** and rises until it forms clouds in the sky. When the clouds become heavy with water **vapor,** the water falls back to the earth in the form of rain or snow. The water returns to the earth, and the cycle begins again.

THE WATER CYCLE

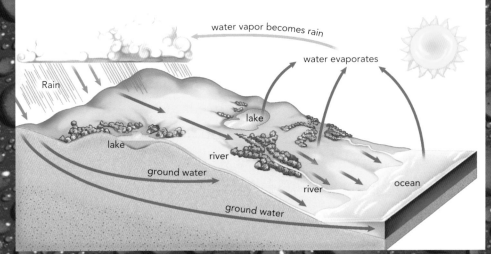

water vapor becomes rain

water evaporates

Rain

lake

lake

river

ground water

river

ocean

ground water

The Coniferous Forest

Coniferous forests grow in cold parts of the world.

The trees that fill a coniferous forest look green even in fall and winter. That is why coniferous trees are also called evergreens. Coniferous trees have thin, waxy needles instead of wide, flat leaves. The needles drop to the ground throughout the year. New leaves constantly replace the ones that fall. Because the wood of many coniferous trees is easier to cut than that of hardwood trees, coniferous trees are often called softwoods.

The cone shape of coniferous trees helps them shed snow and ice in the cold winter months. Coniferous trees also form cones that protect their seeds from cold weather. From the cones comes the name *coniferous,* which means "cone-bearing."

Tree branches, dead needles, and pine cones litter the floor of a coniferous forest. Few living things grow on the forest floor because the coniferous trees keep the sunlight from reaching the ground. The branches, needles, and pine cones of coniferous trees take a long time to decay, so the soil is not enriched quickly. Only

Lichens

Mosses

Liverworts

Lichens, mosses, and liverworts grow on the floor of a coniferous forest.

living things such as lichens (LY kenz), mosses, and liverworts can grow in such a shady place with poor soil.

Owls live and nest in the high branches of the trees in a coniferous forest. They eat birds and small **rodents** such as mice. Other birds that can be found in a coniferous forest include hawks and woodpeckers. The lynx, fox, and wolf hunt small animals like rabbits and weasels. Deer and bear are also found in coniferous forests.

Cones and seeds of a spruce tree

Forest Fire:
Lifesaver or Killer?

Most people think of fire as a terrible tragedy. It's true that fire destroys almost everything in its path. If animals can run fast enough or fly, they can escape fire. But some plants and animals burn and turn to ash. It is this ash that helps the forest. The trunks of trees contain important nutrients. When the trees burn, these nutrients become ash. When ash mixes with soil, it adds nutrients that new plants need in order to grow.

A forest fire also brings sunlight to the forest floor. Soon after a fire, plants send up new stems and leaves. They can do this because their roots do not burn. The new plants make seeds that **germinate** in the rich soil and grow into new plants.

Some trees need the heat of a forest fire to make their seeds germinate. If a forest fire is put out, these seeds will not grow, and the trees will disappear from the forest.

Fire both destroys and helps forests.

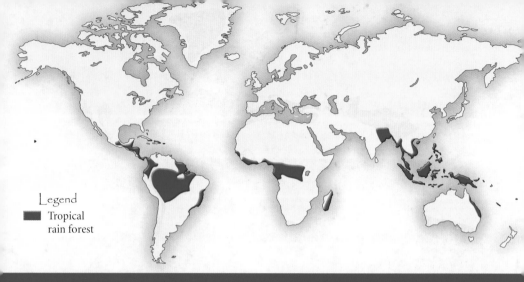

Legend

■ Tropical rain forest

CHAPTER 3

THE TROPICAL RAIN FOREST ECOSYSTEM

In South America a giant river otter ambles up the bank of the Amazon River. The otter has already eaten 9 pounds (4 kilograms) of fish that day but still searches the bank for tasty tidbits. High above, a troop of red howler monkeys jump from branch to branch in the treetops. Spotting a boat on the river, they howl and screech to warn other animals.

Mosquitoes buzz in the shade of the tall trees. Flies buzz around a ripe mango that has fallen to the ground. A large boa slides slowly out of the jungle growth. It slithers toward nearby huts to search for its next meal. Huts mean that people are present. The boa knows that wherever people live, so do mice.

What does a tropical rain forest have a lot of? Rain, of course! Some tropical rain forests are found in Central America and South America. Others are found in Asia, Africa, and some islands in the Pacific Ocean. Each one receives 80 to 100 inches (200 to 250 centimeters) of rain each year. The sun shines for twelve hours a day in a tropical rain forest, so it is a very warm place. A warm, wet ecosystem like this is a good place for many plants and animals to live. The tropical rain forest has more kinds of living things than any other ecosystem.

Trees of the tropical rain forest can grow as tall as 200 feet (60 meters). Ropelike vines called lianas cling to the tallest branches and hang down to the ground.

Clouds cover many tropical rainforests.

Lianas attach themselves to a tree when it is young. The lianas grow taller as the tree grows.

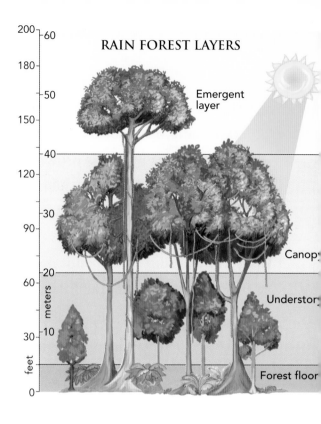

RAIN FOREST LAYERS

Emergent layer

Canopy

Understory

Forest floor

Many animals make their home in the tops of the tallest trees. Harpy eagles can easily spot animals to swoop down upon and capture. Macaws, which are large parrots, also live in the top branches of trees. They must take care to avoid the dangerous harpy eagles that might capture and eat them!

Beneath the top layer of trees is another layer called the canopy. Because the leaves of these trees grow so thickly, little light filters through to the forest floor below. Monkeys, sloths, insects, birds, frogs, and reptiles make their home in the canopy. Small mammals like opossums, anteaters, and porcupines can also be found there. The trees of the canopy provide foods such as fruits, nuts, flowers, and berries.

Young trees and ferns grow in the forest layer called the understory. The air in the understory is damp, and the light is poor. The understory feels much like a steamy bathroom!

Macaw Clay Licks

After dawn, hundreds of macaws arrive at riverbanks made of clay along the Tambopata (TOM buh PAH tuh) River in South America. Then the birds eat small globs of the clay.

No one knows for sure why the macaws eat the clay. Some scientists think the clay has nutrients that the birds need. Other scientists think the clay acts to keep the birds healthy. These birds eat many nuts and fruits. Many of these nuts and fruits have poisons in their shell or skin. Scientists believe the clay removes the poisons in the birds' stomachs before they make the birds sick.

21

Tiny living things called green algae grow in the fur of three-toed sloths. The algae help the sloth hide among the leaves of trees.

The floor of the rain forest bustles with life. One animal that lives on the floor is the capybara (kap uh BAHR uh), the largest rodent in the world. A capybara looks for mangoes or other fruits to munch. An anaconda, a kind of snake, searches for animals to eat. Blue butterflies flitter here and there, searching for nectar.

Even though the tropical rain forest is packed with plant and animal life, the soil is only rich on the top layer. This layer only goes down 4 inches (10 centimeters)! Why is this layer of soil so thin? Living things are eaten so quickly by others that few of them ever get a chance to decay. Because of the shallow soil, the roots of the giant trees spread out very far to get the food they need. Clay lies below the thin layer of rich soil and does not provide as many nutrients as rich soil.

Why We Need the Tropical Rain Forest

When people burn coal, oil, and gas, these fuels give off carbon dioxide into the atmosphere around Earth. The sun's rays can shine through carbon dioxide, but heat cannot escape through it. Too much carbon dioxide in the air causes **global warming**. If global warming continues, ice at the North and South poles will melt. This melting ice could cause flooding. Many scientists are afraid of what else might happen if the atmosphere gets too warm.

The many kinds of plants in the tropical rain forest ecosystem take carbon dioxide out of the air and release oxygen that animals need. The problem is that tropical rain forests are being destroyed each day. People cut them down and burn them down to make farmland or raise cattle. Many groups are working together to save the tropical rain forests that still exist.

CHAPTER 4

THE DESERT ECOSYSTEM

The bright sun beats down on the hot, sandy Sonoran Desert in North America. In the heat of the day, most of the animals seek a cooler, shady place. Some rest under rocks. Others burrow into the sand. Only the cactus stands tall, the water inside it protected by its thick, stretchy skin.

When evening comes, many of the animals come out and hunt for food in the cooler air. Mule deer search for the few plants to eat. A wasp stings and kills a tarantula spider. A kit fox chases a jackrabbit.

A white-tailed antelope squirrel still sleeps peacefully in its burrow. It doesn't realize that a rattlesnake has slipped into its home and lies inches away, waiting.

Sand dunes in the Sahara desert

Life in the desert ecosystem can be harsh. Hardly any rain falls all year. Because the desert receives little rain, few plants grow in this ecosystem. The soil is poor because nutrients are not washed back into the soil.

Deserts in the northern part of the world are cool, but they are still dry. Other deserts are hot. Their air temperature can soar to more than 100° F (38° C), and the soil can be much hotter than the air.

One reason why day temperatures of hot deserts are so high is that few clouds float over the desert. Nothing lies between the desert and the sun, and the desert quickly gets hot. It stays hot until the sun goes down. Then the temperature can quickly fall to the freezing point. It falls quickly for the same reason that it warms quickly—the desert lacks clouds. Without clouds to hold the heat close to the earth, the heat quickly fades.

Flowering prickly pear cactus

Despite poor soil and lack of rain, some plants and animals live in the desert ecosystem. How do desert plants live on so little rain? Some grow very long roots that reach water deep in the ground. Others have many short roots that quickly soak up rain. Desert plants also store water. In addition, they keep water in by closing their tiny holes during the day. Some desert plants have a thick, waxy covering that also helps to keep water in.

Several different kinds of cacti grow in the deserts of North America. Like many other desert plants, cacti have many short roots that spread out to catch the rain quickly when it does fall. They store the water in their trunk, which expands when it is full of water. Prickly spines keep animals from breaking open the cacti and eating the juicy trunk to get water.

When the desert does get rain, cactus plants flower quickly. The flowers make seeds, and insects flock to the flowers and spread the seeds in the soil. The new plants grow. All this can happen in only two weeks!

Most desert animals rarely drink water. They get most of their water from the food they eat. Some animals, like the kangaroo rat, don't drink water at all. This rodent gets water just from the seeds it eats.

The kangaroo rat hides in a burrow under the ground to escape predators. Other animals survive because their coloring blends in with things around them. For example, rattlesnakes have brown scales that blend in with rocks and soil. Rattlesnakes use their rattle to tell other animals to stay away. Rattlesnakes cannot hear, so they don't hear the scary sound they make!

A California desert

Keeping Cool in the Desert

To survive in the desert, animals must keep cool. Most animals spend their days under rocks or under the ground. Reptiles have dry scaly skin that keeps them from losing water. Desert insects have hard coverings that keep them from losing water. Many desert mammals have light-colored fur that makes sunlight bounce off. The jackrabbit and the fennec fox have big ears that help them keep cool. As blood travels through the thin skin of the ears, its heat flows out of the body and into the air.

Jackrabbit

Fennec fox

Legend

Grassland

CHAPTER 5
THE GRASSLAND ECOSYSTEM

In Africa a puff adder lies still in dry golden grass. Its scales in shades of brown blend with the grass around it. An eagle flies overhead, looking for the movement of its next meal, but it doesn't see the reptile. The snake feels the ground shake as a herd of zebras approach. A herd of wildebeests follow the zebra. All slow to a walk and then stop to graze. A lion crouches in the grass and studies the wildebeests. It sees a young wildebeest standing by itself and stares at it hungrily.

In the distance a hyena lets loose its frightening cry. The zebras and wildebeests stop to listen, standing still as statues. Then, without warning, they take off. The lion is left alone to watch the animals fade into the distance.

As its name suggests, the grassland ecosystem contains more grasses than any other kind of plant. The grassland receives more rain than the desert but less than forests. Grasses are one of the few plants that can survive year after year with little rainfall.

The leaves of grass begin to grow just beneath the soil. When the grass is trampled, chewed, burned, or cut, it is protected by the soil and grows back. During the dry season, rain doesn't fall for as long as eight months. The grass turns yellow but still does not die below the ground. When rain doesn't fall, grasses become **dormant**. When they are dormant, they rest and stop growing.

The kangaroo lives on Australia's grasslands.

How Termites Keep Cool

Millions of termites work together to build mounds in the middle of grasslands. Huge mounds can take more than ten years to build. A large nest can reach more than 26 feet (8 meters) tall! Why do termites build big mounds? A thin-skinned termite has little chance of surviving in the hot sun. Made of mud, the mounds keep the termites cool. Chimneys carry air in and out of the nest. Tunnels lead from one tiny room to another. Such a mound can contain as many as 2 million termites!

During the wet season of the grassland ecosystem, the rain falls all at once. Then the grasses grow very quickly. Some of the larger grasses can grow more than 1 inch (2.5 centimeters) in just one day!

Fires occur often in grasslands around the world. The grasses are not killed in the fire, because most growing parts of the grasses lie below the ground.

Burned plants and animals leave important nutrients in the soil, so the soil becomes richer.

With so much grass available, grassland animals have plenty of food to eat. Gazelles, impalas, zebras, and other kinds of grass-eating consumers roam the African grasslands. Meat-eating consumers include lions, hyenas, cheetahs, and leopards.

Wildebeests thrive in the wet season of African grasslands. In some places as many as 300,000 wildebeests gather in a herd. Lions and hyenas hunt these large creatures.

Wildebeests move from place to place, looking for food.

A warm grassland that has a few trees is called a savanna. Africa contains the most well-known savannas. These areas are home to ostriches, zebras, antelopes, rhinoceroses, giraffes, elephants, grasshoppers, and snakes such as the puff adder. Kangaroos hop along the savannas of Australia.

The Acacia Tree

The acacia tree is one tree that lives on the savanna. How does it survive? Sharp thorns keep some animals from eating its leaves. The acacia tree also has a poison. When it is being eaten, the tree shoots the poison to its leaves. When some animals taste the poison, they stop eating and move on.

The North American prairie

One grassland ecosystem has cool temperatures. It is called the **temperate** grassland. With its large open space and rich soil, it makes a good place to farm and raise cattle. In North America, the temperate grassland is called the prairie, and it stretches across the Middle Western region of the United States. Farmers raise cattle on the prairie and grow grains. Wild animals live on the prairie, too. Plant-eating consumers include deer, mice, and rabbits. Consumers that eat other animals include coyotes, bobcats, badgers, and snakes. Hawks and owls also look for small prey to eat.

The Burrowing Owl

The burrowing owl is a grassland bird that lives in an underground burrow. When burrowing owls hunt, they fly to fence posts or other high places and watch for prey. When they see something good to eat, they don't fly over it and grab it with their claws. Their long legs are so fast that they chase it on the ground.

The burrowing owl is in danger of extinction because poisons have killed the grasshoppers that it likes to eat. Farmers use these poisons to protect their crops from the grasshoppers. Farm pets like dogs and cats also sometimes kill these owls.

Endangered
Grassland Animals

African wilc

Cheetah

Even with plenty of food to eat in the grassland, the rhinoceros is in danger of disappearing. Hyenas and lions kill rhinos, and some people hunt rhinos illegally. Hunters kill these animals to sell their horns for thousands of dollars. Many countries are trying to protect rhinos from dying out.

Most cheetahs live only in Africa because they are already extinct in other places. Farmers have shot many cheetahs to protect their farm

Rhinoceros

Sandhill crane

animals. The cheetah is the fastest land animal. It can run 68 miles (110 kilometers) an hour.

African wild dogs have short coats with spots. The ears and noses are dark, and the tail is white at the tip. These dogs hunt large plant-eating animals such as gazelles. They also eat farm animals, so farmers have killed many of them.

Because the wild North American prairie is shrinking , herds of pronghorn deer and bison are in danger of disappearing. Even the prairie dog has become endangered because so much of the prairie has been turned into farmland. Other grassland animals that are in danger of disappearing in North America include the sandhill crane and the red wolf.

Red wolf

Bison

Prairie dog

37

CHAPTER 6
THE TUNDRA ECOSYSTEM

The winter sky above the tundra is pitch black, even though it is noon. From mid-November until the end of January, the sun will not rise. Sixty-six days will pass before the sun reappears. A freezing wind blows across the snow and ice. Lemmings burrow under the snow and feed on the roots of plants. Arctic foxes hunt for their next meal in the snow. If they are lucky, they will find a tasty lemming.

Then summer comes, and the days seem to never end. Even at midnight the sun shines low in the sky. The plants turn green, flowers fill the meadows, and animals fill the wilderness. Caribou return to graze on plants. Brown bears search for berries. Billions of mosquitoes flock to this ecosystem that snow and ice will freeze next winter.

The Arctic tundra looks very different in winter and in summer.

The tundra ecosystem is cold and dry. Rain and snow only bring 4 to 20 inches (10 to 50 centimeters) of water a year. Below the top layer of soil lies frozen subsoil that never thaws, so the root systems of plants are not very deep. When water falls on the top layer, it cannot sink into the frozen subsoil. Soft, watery places called **bogs** form on the surface. Many plants grow around these areas of water. The largest area of tundra in the world lies in the Arctic. At its center lies the North Pole. The Arctic tundra lies so far north that it is cold most of the year.

Animals that live in the Arctic tundra must be able to live through long, cold winters. All of the Arctic tundra mammals have thick fur. Some build up layers of fat that keep them warm. Polar bears, Arctic foxes, wolves, and Arctic hares all store fat under their thick fur.

Some Arctic tundra mammals, such as the Arctic ground squirrel, burrow in the snow and sleep for long periods of time. Because they are not moving, they save energy and don't need much food or water. Other mammals stay awake in winter and eat the little food they can find. Musk oxen look for plants. Arctic foxes and wolves hunt for smaller animals to eat.

Musk oxen do not migrate. They are quite comfortable living in the long cold winters of the Arctic.

When the warm summer months arrive, the winter snow melts. The plants peek through the soil, and photosynthesis begins. When the plants return, so do more animals. Many animals live in the tundra only during the summer. Caribou and birds like ducks, geese, and sandpipers **migrate** south during the cold winter.

Snakes and other reptiles could never survive in the Arctic tundra. Reptiles are cold-blooded and depend on the sun to keep them warm enough to move. The Arctic tundra is simply too cold for them.

White as Snow

The Arctic hare and Arctic fox use **camouflage** to help them hide from other animals. The fur of the Arctic hare and the Arctic fox is white during winter. The white fur allows them to blend in with the snow around them. During the spring and summer, these animals turn darker to blend in with the summer plant life. Scientists think that shorter days and colder temperatures send a message to the brains of the Arctic hare and Arctic fox. Their brains then tell their body to grow white fur.

Arctic hare in winter

Arctic hare in summer

The Snowy Owl

The snowy owl is found mostly in the Arctic tundra, but it has been seen as far south as the state of Georgia. Why does this happen? The snowy owl's favorite food is lemmings. When lemmings are plentiful on the tundra, lemmings have trouble finding food. They then migrate south to find more food. When the lemmings migrate, the snowy owl migrates with them.

Some tundra plants begin growing before spring comes. Sometimes the sun shines through the snow and warms the soil. A layer of snow melts, and a tiny space forms. Then the top layer of snow freezes over again and creates a little greenhouse. Sun shines on the ice and warms the air inside the space. Small plants like chickweed and poppies can grow inside these spaces.

The growing season in the tundra lasts only for 10 to 14 weeks. Plants must grow, flower, and produce seeds in this very short time. Because the sun shines day and night during the summer, the plants are able to do these things.

Arctic tundra plants have developed special features that help them survive. They are small and grow close to the ground because the air is warmer there. Tundra plants also grow a hairy type of covering. The hair helps trap the heat inside the plant. Tundra plants have dark colors, too. Their dark colors help them soak up sunlight and heat up quickly. In addition, many tundra plants grow in clumps so they can stay warmer.

The Tundra Swan

Tundra swans migrate south from the Arctic tundra during the cold months. Swan families fly in groups of 10 to 100 birds. Some swans fly 1000 miles (1609 kilometers) in just one day!

Tundra swans return to the Arctic in summer. There they nest and raise their young. The young swans hatch in June and must grow quickly. They have only a few months before they must make the long trip south.

Why Study Ecosystems?

Of all the creatures on the planet, humans are the most powerful. Humans live in every ecosystem. Sometimes we do not cause trouble for an ecosystem. Sometimes we do. In the early 1900s, about 4000 mule deer lived in the Kaibab National Forest in Arizona. Hunters wanted more mule deer to hunt, so they killed all of the mountain lions, coyotes, and wolves that fed on the deer. Twenty years later, the area had 100,000 mule deer. They ate all the plants. They even ate the bark off trees. Then they began to starve to death. No plants were left for the other plant-eaters, so they went hungry, too.

Upsetting an ecosystem can also hurt the people living in it. For example, scientists worry more about the tropical rain forest than any other ecosystem. People are cutting and burning these forests down to make farmland. Without the trees, rain runs off the farmland and into rivers. The rivers flood and kill thousands of people.

Making changes in one living thing can affect many, many others. By studying how ecosystems work, we learn how to keep them and ourselves safe and healthy.

Glossary

bacteria (bak TIHR ee uh) tiny one-celled living things

bogs (bogz) soft, wet areas near water

camouflage (KAM uh flahzh) coloring that hides an animal

chlorophyll (KLAWR uh fil) a green substance found in green plants

consumers (kuhn SOO muhrz) living things that eat other living things

deciduous (dih SIJ oo uhs) shedding leaves at the end of the growing season

decomposers (dee kuhm POH zuhrz) living things that break down wastes and dead living things

dormant (DAWR muhnt) in an inactive state

ecosystem (EHK uh sis tuhm) a group of living and nonliving things that live together in nature

evaporates (ih VAP uh RAYTZ) changes from a liquid into a gas

fungi (FUN jee) living things that have no green coloring and live on dead or live plants or animals. Molds, mushrooms, yeasts, and mildews are all fungi.